A RISK WORTH TAKING

JESSICA JOYCE

ALSO BY JESSICA JOYCE

1

THIS RECYCLING BIN AND I ARE GOING TO RUMBLE.

"Come on, you big...blue...*asshole*," I grunt, trying to lift the bag full of empty booze bottles off the ground while simultaneously opening the bin lid with my elbow.

Everything is working against me, though. The bag is five million pounds and the wind, which has been picking up steadily over the course of the night, bats its hand over the lid and also into my hair, pulling it across my face.

Then the bag breaks.

I see red—literally, because my hair is red and it's in my eyes. But also figuratively, because nothing is going right tonight.

Goddammit. Goddamn everything. I knew I should've turned down this last gig, if not because I've got a one-way ticket bound for San Francisco tomorrow, then because the venue I'm working at tonight is the same one where my ex and I broke up last New Year's Eve. But *no*, I couldn't help going after one last cash grab before I left.

I knew the venue I'd be working at in advance and it's fine, it really is. Ben and I ended because we grew out of each other. Our last months were a slow slide into the inevitable.

But bumping into memories all over this city presses against a heart that's still a little bruised after nearly a year, even if it's no longer broken. It's one of the reasons I'm leaving—a fresh start, new memories that are just mine to hold.

The freezing, head-clearing air is why I volunteered to tow out the approximately forty thousand empty bottles the employees at this holiday party have thrown down. Being out in this alley now, though, surrounded by a mess caused by my irritation, I wish I'd just stayed inside and let Kaia do the heavy lifting.

With a meditative inhale, I turn to the recycling bin and calmly flip its lid. It bounces against the brick wall behind it, then snaps shut.

"I'm going to kill you," I state, hands on my hips.

"I wouldn't," a voice says behind me. "Recycling bin homicide carries a life sentence in Portland."

I whip around. A white guy with light brown hair stands in the doorway leading back into the venue, the intro to Doja Cat's "Paint The Town Red" leaking around his broad shoulders. It's the fourth time the DJ has played it tonight and we've got two hours left of this thing; I'm going to be hearing it in my sleep for the next three weeks, minimum. That's the least of my worries, though.

The most of my worries is taking the concrete steps toward me, hands in his pockets.

It's the beautiful man I've been slyly scoping all night. The man I'm pretty sure has slyly been scoping me back.

"A life sentence, huh?" I sound stupidly breathless to my own ears, but he's an air-snatcher—an easy half-foot taller than my 5'7, and wearing the absolute hell out of his gray suit. I let my eyes drop down his body, just a flick. When I lift my gaze back to his, he's grinning.

Is this the first time he's caught me checking him out so obviously or the thirtieth? His smile reveals very little.

His expression melts into faux severity, though his eyes

(color undetermined) sparkle mischievously. "You know how seriously Portland takes its recycling program."

"God, well, I'd hate to know the sentence if I went after the compost bin."

He whistles through his teeth. "Straight to hell, I'm afraid."

I laugh, and he does, too, a rich, dark sound that I swear I can taste in the bitterly cold air. His lips are perfect, a bitten pink, fuller on the bottom with a cupid's bow I'd like to trace with my tongue.

The sound of clinking glass breaks me out of that utterly inappropriate thought. I look down at the bottles I kicked in my horny stupor.

Shit. I still have to clean all of this up and Kaia's probably drowning inside.

I sigh, pushing my hair back from my face. "I—"

"Let me help you," he interrupts, stepping forward. "Sorry, I distracted you."

You sure did, I think as he crouches down, the fine fabric of his suit stretching to accommodate the movement. The curved line of his thigh is indecent, the square cap of his knee damn near spiritual.

I drop down beside him to start gathering bottles. "Please don't tell me you heard me yelling at the recycling bin from inside."

He looks over at me. This close, I see his eyes are brown like mine, rimmed nearly black, as dark as the lashes surrounding them. He's beautiful. Who can blame me for sneaking glances all night?

"No, I was escaping a hostage situation," he says. He stands, propping open the bin lid with his elbow and throwing the bottles in.

I grimace up at him. "Sounds serious."

He crouches again, his knee brushing against mine. "Let me

rephrase: small talk feels like a hostage situation when it's with my boss."

"Not your favorite person, I take it?"

"He's at the bottom of the list. Right below my childhood dentist, who traumatized me for all subsequent dental procedures."

My gaze moves to his mouth. He grins, showing off generally straight teeth, though his bottom incisor is a little crooked. Adorable. "I'm sorry you escaped a hostage situation only to stumble into an active murder scene."

"This is a lot more pleasant," he assures me.

I laugh. "Your standards are extremely low."

"Only when it comes to crimes."

I hum and he echoes the sound, making it playful. A cat toying with a mouse. I feel irrevocably caught, especially as the moment extends, stretching into something expectant. Beyond the closed door, the bass pounds, the party raging on. At the end of the alley, cars drive by, wheels slicing over wet pavement. The building across the street is half-heartedly adorned with blinking Christmas lights, and they reflect off the honeyed stretch of his cheekbones.

Since I made the decision to move to San Francisco, I haven't regretted it, but the feeling in my chest right now is something startlingly adjacent to that. I haven't dated since Ben, haven't wanted to. But there's something about this guy that hooked me from the first moment I saw him and it won't let go.

It's a shame I can't explore it.

His eyes move over my face, something in them heating imperceptibly, even as his mouth tilts into an impish grin. "This'll go faster if you actually put the bottles in the bin, you know."

Oh, dear god. We're still surrounded by bottles and I've put exactly zero in the recycling bin. My face explodes with heat, even as I arch an eyebrow. "Bold of you to say that when you've only managed to get three in there so far."

He gathers two handfuls, holding them up. "Excuse you, I can easily handle six."

I look down at the three clutched in my hands. "Unfair hand size advantage."

"I've never had any complaints," he says silkily, standing.

I eye his hands as I stand, too; I imagine he hasn't. He's broad-palmed with long fingers. Hands big enough to curve around a thigh, to hitch it up. That's what he meant, right? No complaints while he's handling someone, moving their body the way he wants it.

My heart beats fast, imagining the ways he'd want my body. *If* he wanted it. "You can't just throw innuendo around a crime scene, Stella."

The name slips out before I can catch it. Kaia and I have been calling him that all night because he snagged that brand of beer his first round, though it's been different each of the five times he's come back to order drinks—always from me.

Surprise flashes in his eyes. "How'd you know my name?"

I rear back. "Your name is *Stella*?"

"My last name," he says, grinning now. "First name Connor."

"Oh. Wow. Well, my coworker and I call people by their drink orders. Mai Tai's a real asshole, by the way."

He throws his head back, laughing. "That's my boss."

I grin, loving the sound of his laughter, even as it's drowned out by the clatter of bottles thrown into the bin. "So, do you order your namesake beer on purpose?"

"That was for someone else," he says, bending down again. "I'm not much of a drinker, especially in situations like this."

I snatch up three bottles of Moët. "What's a 'situation like this'?"

His hand pauses over a Jack Daniel's as he shrugs. A lock of wavy hair falls across his forehead as he gathers his next hand-ful, the Christmas lights across the street tipping the strands in gold. "I like to keep my wits about me with this crowd." His eyes lock with mine as I hold the bin lid open for him. "I don't know if you've noticed, but Mai Tai's not the only asshole among us."

It's true. I bartended my last two years of college and stepped back into it with these private events a few months ago to get some extra cash, so I have plenty of experience with drunk dick-heads. Tonight there's a surplus of them.

"I'm sorry. Working with people like that has to be tough."

Connor raises a shoulder, though his expression clouds over. "I handle it. And hey, escaping from my boss gave me the oppor-tunity to save the recycling bin from an untimely death."

"And me from jail."

That beautiful grin returns. I groan inwardly at how proud I am to have caused it.

My phone vibrates in my back pocket and I pull it out with an apologetic murmur as Connor continues to help. It's a text message from Kaia that simply reads:

?????????

"Shit, I have to hurry. I've left my colleague inside for a long time, and she's probably drowning."

"Go on in." Connor nods toward the door, tossing bottles into the bin. "I've got the rest."

"No, I can't—"

He holds up a hand. "Please. You're doing me a favor. Five minutes out here is five less minutes I have to hear about my boss's dalliance with crypto."

"Are you sure?"

"Desperately."

I take him in for a beat—the earnest set of his eyebrows, the hair that's getting further mussed by the wind. He's so handsome it hurts. I hate to walk away. But I have a job to do before I leave for good and I can't abandon it to flirt with a man who'll forget all about this when he wakes up tomorrow.

"Okay. I—thank you," I say, backing away.

He murmurs "no problem" as I hustle up the stairs.

My hand is on the door handle when he says, "Hey. What's your name?"

I look back at him. A tactical error, because he's watching me with a glint in his eye. I can't tell if it's mischievous or hungry. Or both. I imagine that look in other scenarios, then mentally smack myself.

Not happening.

I swallow hard. "It's Claire. Ashford, since we're handing out last names."

He repeats it like he wants to memorize it and I give him a nod before I slip inside.

He doesn't need to remember it at all. But god, some small part of me wished he did.

2

"YOU BETTER HAVE BEEN SWALLOWED BY A BLACK HOLE OR something, otherwise I'm going to destroy you for taking so long," Kaia yells over the music as I rush behind the bar. There's a line six deep and I wave the next person up, pushing my wind-blown hair behind my ears.

"Get me a glass of the Cab," the guy says to my breasts. I sigh internally, but give him my best customer service smile and get to pouring.

"The bag broke," I say to Kaia as she whips up a Manhattan. "And then Stella came outside."

Her eyes flash over to me, wide and dark, as she hands her customer his drink. "Okay. Intrigued."

I explain it between customers and by the time I'm done, she's vibrating with excitement. "If you don't find that man when this is over, I will never forgive you."

"Kaia, I'm leaving for San Francisco tomorrow. For forever. There'd be no point in starting something tonight even if he wanted to."

"Even if he wanted to," she scoffs. She leans against the bar, raising a black eyebrow. "You're a smart woman and you know when someone is flirting with you. All I do is watch you brutally brush off people throwing their metaphorical underwear at you." She pokes me with a fire-red nail. "You haven't done that with him. You're interested. I can tell."

Connor's handsome face flashes in my mind. I can't deny it. "There's still no point."

"The point is to get a good dicking before you leave."

"I don't need *any* dicking before I leave," I say with a laugh, ignoring the rollercoaster dip in my stomach.

"You are so disappointing," Kaia sighs. Someone steps up to the bar, saving me from the rest of the conversation. But not without her muttering out of the corner of her mouth, "Take a risk."

Her challenge drops like a bomb into my mind, scattering the pieces of my knee-jerk cautiousness.

For so long, my life was a series of safe, measured decisions. One of my earliest memories is staring up at the huge tree in the front yard of my childhood home in Issaquah, Washington, wondering if it was worth it to attempt the climb. Anything could happen: I could fail, I could fall, I could make it to the top and get stuck. When it was time to consider colleges, I wrote list after list, weighing the impact each option would have on my life. It took my parents' encouraging but forceful push to get me to the University of Oregon, a mere five-hour drive from home.

I've spent the majority of my life in that mindset: is it worth it to change? To take that risk? There's a reason my family nicknamed me Claireful. I stayed in safe jobs, walked the most reasonable path. My breakup with Ben took time, too, because it was comfortable. Even if it wasn't good, it was better than upending my entire life.

Until it wasn't.

I had a conversation with my older brother, Tristan, two days before New Year's Eve last year. Ben and I had gotten in a stupid fight over a small thing that had ballooned into something ugly. He'd left me alone in our echoing apartment and I called Tristan, needing reassurance that we were going to be okay. Needing him to lie to me, I guess.

But Tristan is the most pragmatic, zero-bullshit person I've ever known. Deep down, I knew he was going to tell me what I couldn't tell myself. The advice he gave me changed the trajectory of my life.

"What would it cost you to do nothing?" he asked me after I'd unloaded my woes.

I sniffed, wiping at my swollen eyes. "What do you mean?"

"I mean, if Ben comes home and you make up and keep going, what will the cost be?"

"I...I don't know."

"I had an Econ professor once who told us about the cost of inaction. It's natural to think of the risks associated with any big change, like switching jobs or moving or ending a relationship." Tristan's voice took on a meaningful weight. "But it's not as natural for us to think about the risks associated with *not* changing. What are you missing out on if you don't take the job or move across the country? What are you missing out on, Claireful, if you don't get out of a relationship you know isn't working for you?"

I didn't have an answer for him right then, but later, when Ben slipped into our bed after his all-day absence, I started thinking about the happiness I was giving away by staying. Not just mine, but Ben's, too.

We broke up just before midnight while everyone around us counted down, and I started this year with a brand-new perspective.

Kaia has no idea the bullseye she just hit. Now, instead of thinking of the cost of action, I imagine the opposite: what would it cost me to do nothing? To not take a risk that could change my life?

It could cost me everything. Not only with major decisions, but in small moments I let pass me by.

It's not that deciding to indulge in a one-night stand is a life-changing thing, but it could certainly change my night. The cost of not seeing if Connor would be down for it is that I'd never know what his mouth feels like, what he tastes like. I wouldn't know the fun we could have, if our earlier interaction was any indication.

It could be an easy, no-strings thing. One last Portland memory I can tuck into my carry-on tomorrow and take with me.

Across the room, Connor is standing with a small group. The impish smile he wore outside is gone, replaced by an expression that, when no one's looking, is glazed with boredom, maybe even misery. But then his gaze swings to the bar—to me—and the life comes back into his eyes. He arches an eyebrow with a quiet grin.

Hey, he mouths.

Hey, I mouth back and his smile grows. The keen interest in his gaze goes straight to the pit of my stomach.

The cost of inaction would be not getting to see that look up close. It's a cost I could afford, but dammit, I don't want to.

Beside me, Kaia lets out a low laugh. "I swear, if you don't—"

"I am," I interrupt her, uncorking a bottle of Merlot. "I one hundred percent am."

I HAVE NO PLAN IN PLACE TO MAKE THIS HAPPEN, BUT IT TURNS OUT that doesn't matter. By the time Kaia and I are done breaking everything down and settling the final tab, Connor's still milling around with a group of stragglers who clearly don't want to admit the party's over.

He's been watching me, as if he wants to catch me before I leave. And that's exactly what he does as Kaia and I shrug into our coats and head toward the entrance. He smoothly side-steps out of his conversation, intercepting us.

He gives Kaia a friendly smile and a breathless little "hello" before turning to me, his expression turning playful. "We meet again."

"It's getting weird," I agree, my heart thumping hard.

"I was wondering…" He trails off, running his knuckles along the length of his jaw as he seems to consider his words. I watch something fortify in his eyes, which under the brighter house lights are the color of honey shot through with sunlight. They travel over my face, snagging on my mouth, before our gazes catch again. The connection is like flint to steel—the spark of it heats my blood.

"This invitation is going to sound redundant considering… uh, the entire night," he says, "but I was hoping I could talk you into grabbing a drink with me. Or food. Or whatever." He barks out a self-deprecating laugh, his cheeks flushing slightly. I bite back a smile. "Okay, I'm fucking this up, but I'd like to spend some time with you if you're up for it. Preferably not in an alley with garbage."

Beside me, Kaia's silence is piercing.

"We could probably find somewhere with better ambiance," I say.

He nods, mock-serious. "Less crime."

"We-ell…" I teeter my hand back and forth and he laughs, his eyes lingering and warm. "Let's see where the night takes us."

"Sounds ideal," he says, the timbre of his voice dipping almost imperceptibly lower.

Kaia metaphorically karate kicks through our delicious tension. "Well, hey! You two enjoy your drink." The tone of her voice makes it clear *drink* is a stand-in for *fuck*. "There's a big ice storm rolling in later, by the way. Wherever you end up, you might want to stick close to home. You know, just in case you need to hunker down. Together."

There's no way Connor misses her lascivious wink. Then again, there's no way anyone left in this entire venue misses it.

"Thanks for your completely normal care and concern, Kaia," I say loudly, herding her forward. Connor's laugh rumbles through me.

"Wait, I'm not going to see you again!" She turns, pulling me into a tight hug. "Let's hang out if you ever come back to visit."

I'm not planning on it, but I nod against her hair. "Same to you, I'd love to show you around San Francisco."

Kaia leaves us with a wave, disappearing through the front entrance, looking like a retina-burning marshmallow in her neon green parka.

I turn back to Connor, who raises an eyebrow. "San Francisco?"

My stomach dips. Admitting I'm leaving tomorrow is either going to end this or make it even more compelling for him. I desperately hope it's the latter.

"I'm moving," I say, playing with the zipper on my puffy coat. "Tomorrow, actually."

Something that looks like disappointment flashes across his face, but it's so brief I might have misnamed it. "What's down there?"

"A new job," I say. "I...well, I needed a change and this opportunity came along. I have a friend who offered a room in her apartment for a frankly unbeatable price, so I decided to take the leap."

It's a vast oversimplification of the truth: that once Ben and I broke up, all hell broke loose in my mind. I started seeing the ways in which I'd settled everywhere—in the lackluster freelance copywriting gigs I'd taken after finally leaving my mind-numbing corporate job. In the friends who maybe weren't so solid after all, given that they disappeared alongside Ben.

Four months ago, I landed a freelance assignment with a new woman-owned cosmetics company in San Francisco. The work sparked life inside me. It was fun and rewarding and it showed me what I was missing. From the way the creative director was talking, I had a feeling it could turn into a permanent offer, so I started working private events like this one to pad my savings account thanks to a hookup from Kaia. When the offer came, it was a big decision, one that would have scared me away the year before. But post-Ben me felt mostly prepared for the way it would upend my life.

"A leap. I like that." I don't miss the admiration in Connor's voice. "Sounds adventurous."

"I'm excited," I say, letting out a breath before blurting, "a little nervous, too, though."

He spreads his hands in front of him. "Well, I'm somewhat of a moving connoisseur, so if you need any tips, I'm your guy."

We start a slow stroll toward the front door. My coat is thick, but I swear I feel Connor's hand against my back before the slight pressure is gone again. "What exactly constitutes a moving connoisseur?"

"I've lived in six cities since I graduated from college eleven years ago, all for new jobs," he says. I mentally calculate that he must be around thirty-three, four years older than me. "I'm a little, ah, impulsive, I guess. Or adventurous, if you want to position it in a more palatable way." He takes two quick steps so he can open the door for me. As I brush past him, I get a whiff of his cologne, something spicy and dark.

"My nickname is Claireful, so you can guess where I land on the spectrum."

The wind has increased significantly since our tête-à-tête in the alley and as soon as we step outside, it plasters my hair across my face. I paw at it with an exasperated grunt.

Suddenly I feel the gentle sweep of fingers on my skin and my vision clears. Connor is close, facing me, taking such care to get every strand out of my eyes, off my cheeks. He pushes it behind my ears, trapping me in his honey gaze.

"Well, Claireful," he says, and the way he shapes my name makes me shiver. "Taking a leap and moving to a brand-new city is pretty brave to me, and I'm an expert, remember? So maybe your place on the spectrum is further over than you think."

"Maybe," I murmur.

"I could stand to be a little more careful. Or slow down, at least. That's what my parents always told me when I was little and breaking shit left and right, or taking everything at a dead run." His voice is low, his expression morphing into that hunger I saw a glimpse of earlier. "You have any tips for that?"

His hunger feeds mine, stripping away any coyness. "Slow and careful isn't really what I want to be tonight."

His eyes darken, even as his mouth twists with what I can now clearly see is disappointment. "And tonight's all we have, huh?"

"Afraid so," I say.

That mischievous smile curls back onto his face. "I'd better show you a good night, then, so you miss Portland a little when you leave."

"That's a lot of pressure."

He winks. "I'm willing to take it on for you."

I think of the limited number of hours we have until I leave tomorrow. Of the heat that's stirring in my stomach. Lower. I think of the things I'd like to get into with this near-stranger who's somehow a little familiar already. The thought of sitting in some bar surrounded by people feels like a waste.

What is the cost of inaction here, Claire?

"I'm about to be intensely forward," I warn him.

Connor's eyes light up. "The answer is yes."

I laugh, stepping closer. He stills, like he doesn't want to spook me. But I won't get spooked. Not tonight. Not with him.

His mouth parts slightly when our bodies brush, then press

together with more intention. I feel a gentle tug at my hip. His hand, taking a fistful of my coat to keep me anchored.

"Do you have drinks or food or whatever at your place?"

For a second, he's silent, his eyes moving over my face. And then he says huskily, "I have all of that."

I reach down to cover his hand with mine. His knuckles are cold from the air, his cheeks turning pink from the weather or my question. He releases my coat, turns his palm so that it kisses mine. Taking his hand feels like the riskiest thing I've done in years and somehow also the safest.

Our fingers intertwine. Lock into place.

My voice is so soft it surely gets swallowed by the wind. But Connor somehow hears me when I say, "Then let's go."

3

"LET ME TAKE YOUR COAT."

I start to turn, but Connor stops me, his hands cupping my shoulders. I shiver a little when his fingers graze along my collarbone as he helps me out of it. The chill from outside clings to the material and his skin, a goosebump-raising dichotomy to the warmth of his apartment.

The ride to his apartment in Slabtown was a study in over-stimulation: miniature Christmas lights adorned every square inch of our Uber and Mariah Carey's ubiquitous holiday hit was played on a continuous loop, preventing Connor and I from having any kind of meaningful conversation.

I looked over at him at one point to see him mouthing along to the words, bobbing his head with a faraway expression. When our gazes caught, though, he turned the performance up to ten, his grin going megawatt. I laughed and sang along, but my eyes lingered on his mouth, wondering what shape it could take with other activities. He caught me and the mood shifted like a finger snap. His hand slid across the seat between us, catching my fingers under his, squeezing them once and again.

Now that we're inside his home, the anticipation I felt during the ride has ratcheted up to ten. I'm not nervous—once I decide

I want to do something, I'm all in—but wondering what exactly is going to happen makes my mind race with possibilities.

"This can just be a drink, you know."

I turn, watching as Connor shrugs out of his suit jacket, hanging it up in his small hallway closet next to my coat. He's been hiding a white button-down shirt that's unfairly tailored to his body all night. A black belt lays flat against his stomach, his dress pants molding perfectly over the legs I was admiring earlier and what I can now see is a spectacular ass.

I'm transfixed by the curve of it, but Connor must think I'm hesitating. He steps closer, his expression careful. "Seriously. I have some really good alcohol or Sprite or, like, way too many flavors of Bubly. You can drink me out of house and home. Or if you changed your mind at some point during that fever dream of an Uber ride, it doesn't even have to be that."

My heart is beating hard and fast. It feels like I just went for a five-mile run. Like I'm sitting on top of the first crest of a roller-coaster, right before I tip over. "It *was* a fever dream, right?"

"Without a doubt. My head is still spinning," he says, gazing down at me. I'm not sure he's talking about the Uber.

I don't know anything about his apartment other than it's apartment-shaped and there must be a window letting in street light, because his eyes are lit up. He listed out a variety of drinks that sound fine in theory, but that's not what I'm craving right now.

"I don't want a drink," I say quietly.

"Okay," he says, voice dipped low, too. "Whatever you do want, maybe you should start it."

I like the way he says that, with a weight of familiarity, like he knows me already. I like how he puts me in the driver's seat, how he stills as I close the meager distance between us, my fingers wrapping around his wrist. I like the way the breath escapes from between his parted lips, soft and unsteady, as I draw his hand around to the small of my back. His palm fits against the valley of my spine, fingers digging into the dip at my waist.

He holds me tight to his body, but still he lets me lead. It makes me bold and hungry and my hands curl around his neck. His hair is soft when I dive my fingers into it, the nape of his neck hot against the inside of my wrists. And when I tighten my hold, just barely, his expression goes tight with desire, his Adam's apple bobbing along the strong column of his throat.

I grin. He does, too, intoxicated. We don't need a drink when we have this—my hands pulling his head down, his mouth parting into the barest pout as it nearly meets mine. It's a tease at first, our lips just grazing, teeth bared in breathless smiles. Connor hovers a millimeter from me, his gaze locked with mine. His breath fans over my mouth, his bottom lip brushing against mine as he tilts his head. A wave of desire slams through me to almost have him, to know we're about to tip over that first drop.

"You gonna kiss me?" he whispers, his tone equal parts challenge and request.

He asked me, but we both move, meeting in the middle as his hand cinches me tight to him. His other hand cups my jaw as he slants his mouth over mine. At the first touch of my tongue, he lets out a wild groan that takes me from turned on to feral in two seconds flat.

We're moving back from the entryway, Connor lifting me straight off the ground as he continues the kiss, deepening it like some sort of ultra-competent sexual multitasker. He's an unreal kisser—not sloppy but unrestrained, sucking at my bottom lip lightly and then not lightly at all. I wrap my legs around his waist, grinning against his mouth when his hands cup my ass. He squeezes in warning, but I feel the stretch of *his* smile and then suddenly we're laughing into our kiss.

"What?" he asks, breathless, falling gracelessly onto his couch with me straddling him.

I adjust my position, pressing my knees into the leather

cushion at his back. "I don't know, one-night stands are kind of fun."

His eyes crinkle with amusement as his hands shape my hips. "Are they?"

"When they're with you, yeah."

"This is my first one-night stand review, please say more," he says, settling back and lacing his hands behind his head. His expression is open, playful, a direct contrast to the rest of his body, straining in its control.

"To be fair, I have nothing to compare it to."

"No," he groans, his hands dropping to my thighs. "We're going in the wrong direction. Let's talk prowess, kissing expertise, my ability to get rock hard as soon as I get my hands on you."

That's accurate. He's deliciously nestled into the cradle of my legs and I give an experimental roll of my hips, pulling a low moan out of both of us.

"You've really never had a one-night stand?" I ask, nipping at his jaw. His stubble burns against my lips.

He shakes his head, tilting it to give me more room to play. "Can never keep it to one night. Which, you know, is probably a testament to my skills."

I make a path to his ear, whispering, "Or maybe you're just a little barnacle."

He squeezes my ass. "My hands definitely are."

Straightening, I run my fingers through his hair. He tips his head back, his eyes falling closed for a blissful beat before opening again, focusing on me. "What does a one-night stand look like in your book? I don't want to do anything you're not down for."

I play with the first button on his shirt placket, long enough that it slides out, almost of its own volition. Connor looks down, his dark lashes shadowing hollows beneath his eyes, watching as my fingers trail to the next button. That, too, slides out, starting to reveal the topography of his chest—more of that honey skin, a smattering of chest hair.

"I'm down for all of it," I murmur.

"Thank god, because me too." He lets out a breath, running his hands up the outside of my thighs, his gaze wide and earnest on me. "Before that, though...we just met, and we're about to do something pretty intimate—and fucking awesome." He laughs quietly when I do, but then his mouth straightens, his eyes bouncing between mine. "I just want both of us to be comfortable with it, so before we get too far into the awesome stuff, you should know I got tested for STIs after my last partner a while ago and it's all negative. I can show you the results on my phone."

Something tender works its way through me, a slow melt that brings my body closer to his. "I got tested recently, too. I'll show you mine."

"I'd *love* for you to show me yours," he says, voice low, smile soft.

I grin, popping another button on his shirt open. "I'm planning on it."

Connor shifts as if to stand, the muscles in his thighs undulating beneath me. "Let's take ca—"

"In a second," I say, placing my hands on his chest and leaning down to kiss the skin I revealed a minute ago. His heart races underneath my lips. Mine matches it. "I'm having a moment."

"In that case, don't let me interrupt you." His voice is unsteady as he cups my head, tilting his chin so I can kiss up his throat. When I graze my teeth against his skin, he groans deeply. "This is going to be a one-night stand on a technicality, just so you know. If you weren't leaving tomorrow, I'd keep you until you got sick of me."

I try to imagine that and can't, so instead I raise up, let my mouth drift over his, rocking against him, gently at first and then with more intention as his breath shortens. When it's too much, he captures my mouth and kisses me with an intensity that pulls goosebumps onto my skin.

The playfulness from before disappears. I don't know what I like better—impish Connor or this one, whose eyes are blown with lust, pulse beating hard in his throat, his hands taking slow but thorough stock of the shape of me. I decide I like both. I'd probably like all versions of him if we had the time.

Connor pulls me into a deep kiss that leaves me gasping for air, clutching his head as he moves down my jaw, my neck. He nuzzles into the vee of my white work blouse, teeth scraping where my breast starts to curve.

Outside, wind beats against the glass windows, shaking through the potted plants on Connor's balcony. As if on cue, freezing rain starts pelting down. From somewhere far away, I think, *I hope my flight doesn't get delayed.* But when Connor parts my shirt, kissing down my chest until his breath is hot against my nipple through the lace of my bra, I think, *holy hell. Yes I do.*

"You are...fuck," he says, staring at my breasts. It has a wholly different effect than Cab Guy earlier this evening.

Suddenly we're tipping sideways and then I'm below six-plus feet of beautifully made man, my shirt gaping open. His hair is everywhere, his own shirt half unbuttoned, a soft pink smudge of what was left of my lipstick streaked across his sternum. He presses his hips against mine, hissing out a breath as we start to build a rhythm. His hand comes around my thigh, hitching it over his waist as he bends down to kiss me, his tongue sliding in with a wet heat I want to feel so many other places.

"God, I could eat you up," he murmurs against my mouth, biting my lip as if to prove his point. "The first time I saw you across the room tonight, I wanted to."

"Is that why you ordered five rounds of drinks for other people throughout the night?" I ask as I unbutton the rest of his shirt.

"Mmm." His hum is a delicious vibration against my lips. "Just trying to catch your eye, I guess."

"You caught it." I pull his shirt from his pants, parting it and then pushing it off his shoulders. His body underneath is as gorgeous as I imagined—all flat planes and hard curves, with a perfect dusting of hair over his chest and below his belly button. He hovers over me, his biceps standing out in stark relief, collarbone hollowing beautifully as he curves further over me. I'm trapped. I love it. Maybe he'll keep me a little longer.

"I spilled a perfectly good vodka soda when you laughed at one point," I continue, running my hands all over him.

He grins, leaning down to kiss the tip of my nose, and the softness of it startles me, then heats my blood. His expression straightens as his gaze roams over my face. "I could be so fucking reckless with this, but I want to be careful."

My heart drops. "No—"

"No, I mean..." He shakes his head. "I want to be careful with the time we have. I don't want to blaze through it just because I'm fucking desperate for you. I want to..." His body betrays him, hips pushing forward as he groans. "I want to take care, I guess. Of you, and this."

I'm so used to thinking of the word *careful* in how it relates to the way I view the world, historically—with caution, aware of every angle of risk. I never thought of it the way Connor means right now: to literally be full of care. To be thoughtful and attentive. Diligent. When he says it, his eyes on fire, it's a good thing, not something I have to fix.

It was in our exchange about our test results a few minutes ago, too, in that moment he was about to say "let's take care of it." My body knew what it meant before my brain caught up: trust. Permission to let go and fully sink into this night.

I imagine what careful could look like when my hands are on Connor's body. When his body is inside mine. It's so hot, so intensely what I want *right now*, that my skin flushes from my hairline down to my breasts, where he's tracing the curve of one with the back of his knuckle.

I swear he sees the awareness darkening my eyes. A slow smile curls over his swollen lips.

"Will you show me how to do that, Claireful?"

He has no idea how it stitches a little piece of me together, even as it makes me ache. Why'd I have to find him now, when it's too late?

I nod wordlessly, knowing that I'm going to be careful with the time we have, too. I'll hold it in my hands until the very last drop.

4

THIS IS WHAT CAREFUL LOOKS LIKE: CONNOR MURMURING THAT HE wants me on his bed, spread out and naked. Me clutching his hand as he tows me down the hallway after a brief detour to our phones, the rapidly falling rain cocooning us inside the otherwise silent apartment.

It looks like Connor flicking on his bedside lamp, removing his tank watch and placing it on his nightstand alongside a glass of water he brought in for us. The muscles in his back play with the movement, his skin turned as honeyed as his eyes, his hair wrecked by my fingers.

He looks over his shoulder, his keen gaze running over my body. I see the care there. It blows my mind that I woke up this morning not even knowing who this man was and now I'm in my bra in his bedroom, my heart racing, desperate to have his hands all over me.

"I love looking at you but I hate seeing you so far away." He lifts his chin, an invitation to come to him, so I do. When I get within reach, he curls his hands around my hips, towing me in, nuzzling his mouth against my neck. The relief that works its way through me is immediate and huge. "I feel like I ruined the momentum by relocating us."

I wrap my arms around his neck, closing my eyes. "No, it's perfect. You're just so nice to look at. I wanted to check you out before we got up to things."

"You didn't get enough of that earlier?" His muffled voice is full of amusement.

"You weren't shirtless earlier."

He hums, sucking at a spot just below my jaw. His hands get restless, running up and down the valley between my hips and ribs as he bites gently, then sucks again, making a delicious upward path. My skin cools in the patches he leaves behind but my blood goes molten when he whispers in my ear, "Show me how to be careful with this. I want it so fucking bad."

I turn my head and show him with my mouth, my tongue, my hands on his ass as I pull him flush against me. He groans softly, reaching up to frame my face in his hands, his fingers tangling into my hair. We kiss like this for minutes—deep, searching ones that feel like their own conversation, playful, plucking ones that make us smile against each other's mouths before it circles back to an intensity that has Connor shifting his hips into me.

When I push him onto the bed and climb over him decades later, he stares up at me, twisting my hair loosely in his fist. I kiss down the center of his chest where his heart is flying against his ribs, totally unrestrained. I press a *shhh* into his skin before trailing down to his stomach, pulled tight with the anticipation of where I'm headed. My palm stays flat over his left pec, my thumb tracing over his nipple while I kiss the skin above his waistband, until his heart shifts into a rhythm that's heavy but slower.

Connor is silent, mesmerized, lips parted as I rise to my knees. He watches avidly while I unbuckle his belt and unzip his pants, an incredible feat given how tightly the material is straining.

"I want you to," he breathes. "Holy shit I want you to, but you don't have to. It's called a job for a reason."

I laugh, pulling his pants down his hips. He's wearing boxer briefs that showcase the mouth-watering shape of him and I pull those off, too, exhaling slowly when he's naked. There's something about being in my bra and pants and having Connor completely bare. It feels like power he's handed over.

"It's not a job," I assure him, wrapping my hand around the rigid base of him, leaning down to kiss the head. I murmur against his skin, "I'll be careful."

"Oh fuck," he breathes. He gathers my hair in his hands again, making a loose ponytail so he can watch as I taste him for the first time—of how many? Two? What can we fit into this night?

I push the thought away, concentrating on the weight of him against my tongue, the clean taste of his skin mixed with his more elemental flavor. It's been a while since I've done this and it's a rush to hear the shaky pulls of his breath above me, to feel the miniscule shift of his hips. He's holding himself back, trying to be careful in the way we don't need right now. I take him deep, telling him without words that he can break himself open.

"Oh fuck," he says again, voice and thighs trembling. His fingers tighten in my hair, hips starting to move in a steady arc.

He only lets me do this for a minute, maybe two, before his fingers are scrambling along my neck, my shoulders, cupping them to pull me up his body. He rolls me onto my back, kissing me with a wildness that makes me gasp. I'm naked in literal seconds, so quickly that I can't help laughing.

"What happened to careful?" I tease.

"I will be, promise." Connor grins, a bare, wicked thing, and then he's traversing down my body.

He takes his time. His hands shape my breasts and he watches his work before appraising me to see the pressure I want. I squirm into his touch when he keeps it light and playful, groan when he licks my nipple and then grazes it with his teeth. I'm so sensitive that I don't need much. Connor adjusts until it's perfect, until I'm breathless.

"Yeah," he says, "That's what you like."

All I can do is hum in response and he grins. Murmurs how good I taste there, how good I feel, how fucking *good* it is, *right, Claireful?* I nod, clutching at his hair as he moves lower, insinuating himself between my legs. He kisses the inside of my left thigh, making it shiver when his tongue runs over my goosebumps. He does the same with the right, sucking at the skin, pulling back to take in the wetness he's created there and then at the juncture of my thighs. His mouth hovers over me for a beat, for two, his eyes locked with mine.

Then he licks me and a million tiny sparklers go off inside of my body. My hips lift and we both groan as he cups my ass, bringing me closer, increasing the pressure of his mouth before backing off, making it so gentle. He repeats the whole circuit, sighing like he's enjoying the most delicious treat.

My fingers tighten in his hair and he lets out an excited murmur, closing his eyes as he tastes me over and over again. I get there so fast it'd be embarrassing if I didn't know it turned him on so much. His cheeks are flagged with color as he slides one finger inside me and then another when I ask for it. His hips move in time with the rhythm I'm building against his mouth.

He pulls back, lips damp, his tongue touching that cupid's bow. "I could do this for hours. You taste so fucking good, but you're going to come, aren't you?"

"Be less good at it if you want me to last longer," I gasp out, putting my right hand over his left, which is clutching my thigh. He laces our fingers together.

"It's okay," he says in a soft, evil little croon. His lips stretch into a satisfied grin. "I'll do it again. Just give it to me now, okay?"

It sounds like a request, but in reality he doesn't give me a choice. His mouth descends on me again, his brows crashing together as he pushes me to the edge, then nudges me over so swiftly with his tongue and fingers that my moan catches in a bitten off inhale. When I come, it's with a shocked, fractured sound.

Connor groans triumphantly, working me so well that it extends my orgasm into a blissful, rolling wave that dissolves all of my bones. He presses a kiss to each of my shaking thighs, then crawls over me, reaching into the drawer of his nightstand.

Watching him roll the condom on should be perfunctory, or at the very least awkward given that his dick and I are newly acquainted. Instead, I'm transfixed, the high I was coming down from doing a swift U-turn. Maybe it's the slight shake of his hands, the pinch of his brows, or the way he looks at me when he's done, with a small grin that in no way hides how big his need is.

"Good? Or do you need a breather?" he murmurs, kneeling above me. He runs his hands up my thighs, curving his palms around my hips. His thumbs circle my hip bones in a soothing, intimate rhythm.

"No, I'm amazing. Get to it, Stella."

His laugh is quiet as his expression heats; it melts over me when he stretches his body against mine.

If there's anything I've learned in this short time with Connor, it's that there's no guile to him. He's playful, thoughtful, and sweetly intense in equal measure; none of it is held back or artificial. It's probably the least careful thing about him, that he hands over his emotions like this. It makes me feel safe with him. I can be careful or not and it doesn't matter. He's right there, showing me his entire hand.

Right now, it's clear he's lost in his need. He reaches between us, guiding himself to me. I tilt up and our hips rock together to bring him inside, so slowly it makes me pant. He props an elbow on either side of my head, his hands cradling my crown as he leans down to kiss me with a groan that gets deeper with each thrust of his hips. When he bottoms out, he exhales sharply against my cheek, his fingers gripping my hair.

"God..." he trails off, adjusting his stance so he can push even deeper. He holds us there, gazing down at me with the tiniest spark of an emotion neither of us will ever get to name. "I want to go slow, but—"

"Don't." I run my hands over his back.

He keeps it measured despite my request. "Will you stay after this?"

"Yeah," I sigh out, pressing my thighs to his arching hips.

His pace increases, but barely, an unbearable taste of what he can do. "You'll let me keep you up all night?"

"You'd fucking better."

"Wow, a threat has never made me so hard," he says, grinning when I do, groaning when I pull him down for a kiss. He tastes me, sucking at my bottom lip before he gets onto his knees, bracketing my hips with his hands. He's faster now, his thrusts harder. His eyes go hazy and heavy watching my body take him.

It's intensely good in a way that it's never been before, because it's full of care but it's reckless, too. It's a revelation that those two things can exist at the same time. That they can make it even better.

I want him to know the care can be unchecked. It can be wild and fast and messy. I want it and I know he does, too.

I pull him down to me again, lick at his jaw and then scrape my teeth against the sharp edge of it. He groans, so loudly I wonder if his neighbors will hear. I grin against his skin and then lift up so I can murmur in his ear, "Go."

He knows exactly what I mean and clearly needed to hear it because he pushes into me, his rhythm turning quick and so deep that my bones rattle. He grips my thigh with one hand, the other braced against the mattress. His breath puffs over my lips, my cheek, my neck as he buries his face there.

He comes back for my mouth almost immediately, kissing me as hard as he fucks me.

"I want you to come again," he pants out when we've been at it for minutes, our skin slick everywhere. "Will you touch yourself? I want to see what that looks like."

When I reach between us he groans, watching with fever-bright eyes as my fingers circle where his mouth was not long before. The thick stretch of him inside me, the way he's watching me, the movement of his body and the way he grits his teeth to wait for me—all of it coalesces into a feeling that turns around to break me all the way apart.

"Fuck, I feel you coming," he gasps from somewhere far away, but then he's right there, his tongue sliding in against mine as he comes, too, pressing into me once, twice, again and then again. He rides me through the pulses of my orgasm, through his, with a groan that's nearly disbelieving.

Finally, he gathers me to him, feeding me an aching, satisfied sound, an echo of what his body just wrung out of me.

"Holy hell," I pant. My fingernails are halfway into his heaving back. Even now, as we come down, our hips are rocking together, slow now. Careful.

Connor lifts up, staring down at me with a slackened, swollen mouth. "Holy hell," he echoes. "I think I blacked out."

I laugh, out of breath, pushing at his chest. He shakes his head, a soft, incredulous smile breaking over his face like sunlight.

"Why'd it take you so long to get to me, Claire Ashford?" he murmurs, pushing a strand of damp hair off my cheek.

My heart soars into my throat. "I could ask you the same thing."

I assume the conversation's over when he kisses me, his hand so gently cradling my cheek, and then climbs out of bed to go to the bathroom. But minutes later when we've both cleaned up and are back in bed, teeth brushed, Connor pulls me close.

"It's rude of you to be moving tomorrow," he says conversationally, his lips brushing against my forehead.

I pull back, arching an eyebrow at him. "It's rude of you not to live in San Francisco. We could've met at a Christmas party there. Our one-night stand could've been a three-nighter."

"Six," he counters.

"I could be talked into five," I muse, running my fingers through his hair. His eyes drift shut, a smile passing over his mouth like smoke.

"Our numbers don't match."

I *would* take six, but I don't say it out loud. In the end it doesn't matter, though having only one night suddenly feels like a gross injustice. It doesn't sour the sex we just had, not even a little bit. But it makes it taste a little bittersweet.

"How many hours do we have?" Connor murmurs, his voice heavy with the sleep that's pulling at me, too.

My eyes slide to the digital clock on his nightstand. It's nearly two. "Ten. Eleven if I'm really feeling the YOLO holiday spirit."

"I'll drive you," he says, pulling me closer. His mouth drifts against mine, softer than a dream. "And we'll just have to put all of those eleven hours to good use."

He's asleep ten seconds later. I use another precious minute to watch him, taking in the smile that doesn't leave his lips even when he's unconscious, before I close my eyes, too.

5

As it turns out, Connor really is a barnacle. I wake up twice in the night, the first time because his arm and thigh are dead weights over me, pinning me to the mattress, and the second time because he's unconsciously helping himself to a handful of my boob. But when I wake up for good, I'm alone, and it takes me a moment to place myself in his space.

I blink at the dresser to the right of the bed, taking in the clearly well-loved stack of thrillers, biographies, and travel guides, and the Polaroid camera serving as a makeshift bookend. He has two framed pictures on the wall above, schematics of what look like baseball stadiums. There's a moderately healthy Ficus in the corner, a laundry basket with some clothes tossed in haphazardly, and hiking boots thrown to the side of it.

The man himself is straight ahead, standing in front of a floor-to-ceiling window, his back to me. Beyond him, the sky is an opaque dove gray.

Even from here, I can see the soft pink half-moons my nails made along his shoulder blades earlier. My cheeks flush as I let my eyes wander over the rest of him. In the weak light, he's rumpled and beautiful, naked except for his boxer briefs, his hair wild from our night together.

I must make a noise—a lust-drunk sigh, most likely. He looks over his shoulder, his eyes soft and slumberous. "Morning, sleepyhead. It's a mess out there. I've seen three cars go sliding down the street from all the ice."

"Shit." I reach over to disconnect my phone from the charger he let me borrow. "I should check my flight."

Connor glances out the window. "You should definitely check your flight. I'll be shocked if it's on time."

My heart kicks up at the implication of that—and the note of hope in his voice.

I can't deny it mirrors the feeling growing in my chest. What if this doesn't have to be over yet? It's delaying the inevitable, but I've never wished harder for an inconvenience.

I pull up the airline app, typing in my information. And there in bold letters: CANCELED.

My body gives a Super Bowl-worthy performance at the news: adrenaline crowd-rushing through my veins, horn-heavy music playing riotously in my heart, confetti cannons bursting in my lungs and brain.

I look at Connor, who's still standing by the window. He probably thinks he's playing it cool, but his eyes are wide with anticipation, his fingers fidgeting with the hem of his underwear.

"My flight's canceled." I say it as evenly as I can, but my mouth betrays my words, pulling up into the goofiest smile that's ever existed. An easy entry into *The Guinness Book of World Records*.

Except that Connor snatches the title away from me when what I've said sinks in. He covers the distance to the bed in two long strides, crawling onto it with an expression that I can only describe as elated and smug. He tackles me, ignoring my shriek of protest, pinning my wrists to the mattress with an exaggerated growl.

"Your flight's canceled," he murmurs, his eyes on my mouth.

I lick my lips, smirking when his part. "It is."

"Sorry."

"Liar," I say, squirming underneath him.

He grins, pushing his hips into mine. "Caught me. Are *you* sorry?"

"I probably should be, but no. I'm not."

It feels strangely like a mutual confession. We've already admitted we'd spend more time together if we could, but that was when it was a futile wish. Even if it's just one more day, now this is real. A choice we're making.

Connor repositions to his side, propping himself up on an elbow. I shift so that I'm facing him, leaning into his touch when he pushes my hair behind my ears.

His gaze focuses on the path his fingers make. "If you want, my apartment is yours until you have to go. Although, I guess you have your own? Unless you've moved out already."

"I have a studio in Southeast Portland, but it's basically empty. I put all my stuff in a moving pod a couple days ago. The company was going to drive it down this week, but I guess the timing of that is up in the air if the roads are a mess." I rub my forehead, my list of to-dos growing by the second. "I'll have to figure out all the logistics."

He nods, then frowns. "Wait. If your stuff's all packed up, where were you planning to sleep last night?"

"My next-door neighbor is a friend and let me borrow their air mattress. I was going to camp out, make a whole adventure of it."

A tiny grin plays across his mouth, his honey eyes warm. "See? Told you you're adventurous."

"Does sleeping on an air mattress count?"

"It all counts, Claireful," he says and my heart grows three sizes. "Luckily, though, you got the upgrade from me."

I wiggle my eyebrows lasciviously. "In more ways than one."

I get a wicked laugh for that, but his expression straightens out, softens as the seconds tick by and we get caught in a quiet moment. Through the window, there's a cacophony of honking, but we're cocooned away from that reality, at least for a while.

It's going to be hard to leave, even with more time. Maybe especially with it.

Connor must see it written on my face. He leans in, brushing his mouth against mine. I curve my palm against his whiskered cheek, letting myself get woozy with his touch.

"Will you stay?" he asks quietly after a lingering minute.

There's no other answer that makes sense. I nod and he sighs, a stripped-away sound. He leans in again, feathering open-mouthed kisses along my jaw, down my neck, sucking at the notch of my collarbone. In seconds, his body is pressed against mine, his skin chilled from the morning air. It doesn't take long for me to warm him up, though, to strip his boxer briefs off and wrap a hand around him. He lets out a happy, hungry sound, pressing his face into the curve where my neck meets my shoulder, thrusting slowly into my fist. He grips my ass and then I'm on top of him and we're rocking together, creating a friction that gets me impossibly wet and him impossibly hard.

Once he's donned a condom, he slides inside me like we've done this a thousand times before. I let myself imagine lazy mornings like this, sex bookended by easy conversation. I hold onto the wish as tightly as Connor grips my hips to set our pace.

Things get urgent quickly. He puts me on my hands and knees, presses his chest to my back, moving my hair so that he can kiss my neck as he thrusts into me again and again. I press a palm to his headboard, feeling stretched tight, pulled apart, wanting it to last as much as I need the relief he's going to give me. He tells me he'll take care of me and then does, fingers circling just above where he moves inside me. He whispers how much he wants this, how unreal it is, then feeds me his sounds as he comes. I let myself get swept up in it, let myself pretend, because there's no risk when it only lives in my head. What does it hurt?

Only my heart, just a little bit.

THE REST OF THE MORNING IS FILLED WITH PHONE CALLS. I MANAGE to get a flight for Monday, two days from now. There's no issue with the timing job-wise since I'm staying remote until the new year. The moving company expects they'll be able to deliver the pod to my new place by Thursday, which is more than doable. I also check in with my landlord, who assures me I can turn in my keys a couple days late.

"Are you sure it's okay that I stay until Monday? I've completely infiltrated your life," I say once I've texted my friend, Leigh, to let her know I'll be there a couple days late.

Connor arches an eyebrow at me from the stove, eggs hissing in a pan in front of him. "Trust me, the infiltration is welcome. And anyway, I was the one who offered. So yes, I'm sure."

I smirk. "Yeah, you seemed sure earlier."

Connor throws me a look, then turns off the burner and sets his spatula down, skirting the breakfast bar where I'm seated. When he gets to me, he slides his hands over my knees and parts them, stepping between my legs. My skin blooms with goosebumps. I'm not a sexually insatiable person typically, but Connor is turning me into a walking erogenous zone.

"The sex is...fucking awesome." He lets out a breath, his gaze going hazy. He blinks back to me, grinning unabashedly when I laugh. "But that's only part of it. You're fascinating and beautiful and you give really good banter."

"Right back at you."

"Comes naturally," he says with a wink before sobering. "I *like* you, Claire. Probably more than I should, given the circumstances. I'd have taken two more hours with you. I'm sure as hell going to take two days."

I wrap my arms around his waist, laying my cheek against his chest. "Just tell me if it's too much."

He presses a kiss to my hair. "I will, but it won't be. Same goes for you, okay?"

Not likely, I think.

When he's done cooking, Connor brings our breakfast plates to the living room and I carry our coffee. If you put the two of us together, we'd be fully clothed—I'm decked out in his University of Michigan shirt, the state in which he grew up and went to school, and he's upgraded to a pair of gym shorts that hug his ass reverently as he bends over to plug in the lights on his Christmas tree.

He straightens and catches me staring, smirking as he takes his seat next to me. I'm not even sorry; it truly is a top tier ass.

Our conversation meanders easily while we eat. He tells me a little more about his work as a senior product manager and how unhappy he's been with the company he's currently at, though he moves us on to lighter subjects quickly—namely, that he's considering adopting a senior cat named Jimbo. I list off all the weird names I've given my pets over the years and we agree Notorious C.A.T. (Kitty for short) is the winner. We also discover we both have two older brothers. His are still in Michigan and I have one, Gavin, in LA, while Tristan's in Seattle, but we agree they're way too dedicated to Big Brothering from a distance.

"What does your family think of your move?" Connor asks as we settle back, sipping our coffee.

"They're excited. They've always encouraged me to break out of my 'comfort zone,' as my mom prefers to label it."

His gaze is steady on me. "What would *you* label it?"

I raise a shoulder. "Scared, maybe? Or too comfortable with being comfortable, at least until this year." I tell him about that transformative conversation with Tristan and all the changes

I've made since, nervously at first, because it's a lot to tell a virtual stranger (*who's literally been inside you*, my brain reminds me). But Connor is quiet through it all, listening intently.

"Once my move solidified, it was a huge weight off my shoulders," I say. "I like the idea that I get a fresh start somewhere new. I've spent a lot of time this year figuring out who I am, as cheesy as that sounds—"

"It doesn't sound cheesy at all," he says, running a hand over my knee.

I swallow, looking at his fingers pressing soft divots in my skin, then meet his eyes again. "I never thought I was the type of person who was brave or adventurous, but you used both of those words with me last night and I think you're right, actually. It's an act of courage to take a chance on something. Last year's Claire had it in her, she just didn't know it."

"But this year's Claire does," he says softly.

"And next year's will, too."

The words seem to hit him somewhere tender. He takes my coffee cup and places it alongside his on the table, then leans forward to cup my jaw, the leather groaning beneath him. His eyes move over my face before he closes the scant distance between us, grazing his mouth over mine. It's the quietest kiss I've ever had, just our mingled exhale, the scrape of my fingers over his stubble-roughened cheek.

"That got heavy for no reason," I whisper when he pulls back, still holding me in the palm of his hand.

His laugh brushes over my cheek. "I started it."

Maybe so, but I dove right in. Even though Connor handled it perfectly, I'm feeling exposed. "Have you ever lived in San Francisco, Mr. Six Cities and Counting?"

He leans back, accepting the shift in mood as easily as he seems to accept everything else. "Never lived there. Visited a handful of times, but—"

I perk up, intrigued by his sudden conversational brakes and the stain of pink on his cheeks. "What?"

"No, nothing."

"You can't do that," I say, scooting closer. "That's against the rules."

"What rules?" he asks with a laugh, scratching uncomfortably at his jaw.

"The rules I just made up in my head."

"What are the other rules?"

"They're filthy."

That gets his undivided attention. His pupils expand, a hungry look replacing the embarrassed one. "Tell m—"

"You have to tell me yours first."

He scrunches his nose, an adorable move that probably got him out of trouble nine times out of ten when he was little. "Okay, well...I have this dream job. Down in San Francisco, I mean. And I had it before I met you, by the way. I don't want you to think I'm Single White Male-ing you or something."

"Considering I've known you a total of twelve hours, I can't imagine you'd come up with something that fast."

"I don't know, this brain is firing on all cylinders twenty-four-seven."

I push at his shoulder. "Tell me."

He sighs, his impish grin fading. "Have you ever heard of that travel app, Where To Next?"

"Of course."

"One of their co-founders left a few years ago, this guy named Theo Spencer. He was their CFO and I've been low-key stalking him since *Forbes* did a profile on him."

"Fanboy behavior," I say affectionately.

He groans, squeezing my thigh. "I know, I know. He's a super smart guy, though, really passionate about environmentally and socially responsible travel. His wife's a photographer who had a whole viral moment on TikTok back in the d—" He waves his hand in the air. "Anyway, he started a sustainable travel company and I'm fucking desperate to work for him."

My heart starts banging out an odd tattoo. "Why don't you?"

"Well," he says, his mouth twisting wryly. "The position doesn't exist. Yet, at least. I assume he'll expand. He accepted my request on LinkedIn a couple months ago and I have alerts on for new job postings. I'm just waiting and hoping at this point."

"Wow." My brain is racing ahead, painting a picture of what that could look like for him. For me.

"Yeah. We'll see what happens, but either way, I can't stay where I am indefinitely." He shakes his head, gazing out the window streaked with rain. "I feel like I've bounced around trying to find something that feels right. And even though this isn't mine yet, it feels right." Our gazes catch, lock into place. "You know what I mean?"

I nod, my mind crowded with words I have no earthly reason to say, or even feel.

"If I ended up down there, I just want you to know—" He breaks off, huffing a frustrated breath. "I'm going to say it wrong."

I can imagine the shape of his thoughts, likely puzzle pieces to mine. "I think I'll know what you mean."

"I wouldn't expect anything, is all. From you. That's why I got all weird before. I didn't want to say all this and then have you feel some undue pressure from me. I respect what you're doing so much, forging out on your own like this. Believe me when I say I get it."

"I know," I murmur. "I don't feel that way at all, for what it's worth."

He nods, biting at his lip nervously. "Who knows, anyway? Right now, it's just a dream."

I run my fingernails up his thigh, watching the skin shiver and rise with goosebumps. "It's a nice one."

It's as close as I can get to admitting just how swept up I am in this.

After a beat, he says, "C'mere."

His voice is low, nearly drowned out by the freezing rain that starts pinging against the window. I crawl onto his lap, smiling when his hands dive underneath my shirt to get to bare skin.

He looks like he's going to say something serious, but then his eyes clear, his face lighting up with a wicked grin. "Remember how you were going to tell me those other rules?"

My blood heats. "Mmhmm."

"I'm cashing that in now. But you have to whisper them all in my ear."

"Do I?" I ask silkily.

He nods, a lock of hair flopping onto his forehead. "And I'm sorry to tell you we have to actually do each one before we can move onto the next."

"There are rules for our rules?"

"There are," he says, molding his hands over my hips, my ass, already shifting restlessly beneath me. "So tell me the next one."

And I do, reveling in his shiver, laughing when he lays me out to get to work.

6

"IT LOOKS PERFECT."

"No, it's wonky on the right side, can you just—"

"If you say 'move it up a little' again, I'm going to body slam you."

Connor looks over his shoulder, his hand extended toward the tape holding down the gold "H" in our HAPPY NEW YEAR banner. A mischievous light enters his eyes.

"Move it up a little," he says smoothly. "On that side, please."

I charge him, though our contact is less body slam and more a mess of exasperated laughter and clashing limbs. I wrap my arms around his waist, pushing him up against the wall. His *oof* vibrates into my chest.

"I know exactly what kind of kid you were, you little button pusher," I say, digging my fingers into his side just to feel him squirm. I found that sensitive spot last night. "We've adjusted the banner, like, thirty-eight times."

"Thirty-eight times? Exactly thirty-eight?" He grins, framing my face so he can squish my cheeks, silencing my rebuttal. "I may be a button pusher, but you're an egregious number inflater."

"You had no qualms when I inflated my orgasm count this morning," I mumble around puffed lips.

His eyes narrow as he releases me. "That's because you said I've given you sixty-nine orgasms in the past thirty-six hours. Firstly, I'm never going to ignore a sixty-nine reference and secondly, I know that you meant *in your heart* you feel the quality of orgasms I've given you are equal to a quantity of sixty-nine."

I smile indulgently. "And *in my heart*, I feel that the number of times we've adjusted this banner is thirty-eight."

He's fighting a grin so hard that his cheeks are shaking. With as much dignity as he can muster (which is very little considering he's wearing a HAPPY NEW YEAR headband, complete with light-up disco balls) he says, "This New Year's Eve party is very important, ma'am. If our banner's crooked, it'll look like an amateur effort."

"It's December fifteenth and we're the only two people attending this party, *sir*," I say, flicking one of his disco balls. "The banner stays."

He narrows his eyes. I narrow mine back. And then we break into twin smiles, meeting in the middle for a swift kiss.

"In that case," he says against my mouth. "I think we're ready to rage."

The idea came to us last night. We spent all day squirreled away in Connor's apartment, finding ways to amuse ourselves, starting with making the other watch our all-time favorite Christmas movie (*While You Were Sleeping* for me and *The Muppet Christmas Carol* for him, which is just...so precious). Later, we pulled out Connor's dusty old karaoke machine to (badly) serenade one another. He was devoted to Journey, while I courageously chose the belters: Whitney, Mariah, Celine. We only stopped when his neighbor banged on the ceiling.

"Some people don't recognize raw talent," Connor muttered, genuinely insulted.

My stomach was still aching from laughter when we climbed into bed and he covered me with the delicious weight of his body, moving inside me with such perfect intensity that the smile I'd been wearing all day wiped clean. It was so good between us, so easy, steeped in that specific blend of care and recklessness Connor seemed to awaken me to.

After, when my heart rate had finally regulated itself from two stellar orgasms and I'd returned from the bathroom, I tucked myself into his arms, watching the occasional reflection of headlights arc across the wall as the world moved on outside.

"What are you doing for the holidays?" I asked, pressing a kiss to his salty, damp skin.

"Going to Michigan," he nearly slurred, huffing when I laughed at how dopamine-drunk he sounded. "I go home every year and stay through New Year's. My mom puts on a raucous party."

"I bet that's fun."

"Oh yeah, the kids stay up 'til midnight and absolutely lose their shit. My brothers and their partners put them to bed at 12:01, then stay up 'til three getting sloppy." Connor's laugh rumbled into my chest as he tightened his arms around me. "And then the kids wake them up at the ass-crack of dawn and all the parents hate their lives while I sleep off my hangover, blissfully child-free."

I smiled, imagining it. It sounded perfect. "I always spend Christmas with my family up in Issaquah, but I never stay for New Year's. I'm going to a party with friends in San Francisco, for which I'm sure I'll barely make it to midnight."

"Any big plans for a midnight kiss?" His voice was even and light, but I heard the uncertainty beneath it.

I leaned back to find his eyes fixed on me, glittering in the near darkness. "I think I'm full up on stranger kisses for this year," I said, brushing my nose against his, biting against a smile at his soft exhale. "Probably full up for the first few months of next year, too."

"Funny, I was thinking the same thing," Connor murmured just before he closed the distance between us. He cupped my cheek as his tongue slid in against mine, warm and slick, dragging up memories of the same sensation between my legs not an hour ago.

"Let's have our own New Year's party," he said after a few minutes of wonderfully indulgent making out. "We can pick up some decorations at the corner store down the block tomorrow. Make it a thing."

"A *thing*?"

"Yeah, you know, countdown, dancing, confetti and shit." He shook me gently, eagerness radiating off him. "C'mon, you know you want to."

I did and so here we are, with our slightly crooked banner and confetti on the ground, which Connor will no doubt be vacuuming up for months to come. But I like that he'll have a lingering, tangible memory of me. If I dropped extra handfuls behind his bookshelf, who could blame me?

I have no clothes other than my work outfit from Friday and Connor demanded a black-tie affair, so I borrow a white button-down and belt it with a black silk tie, just to be thematic. While I relocate to the bathroom to fix my hair and apply the lipstick I found randomly surfing in my bag, Connor bangs around in his bedroom. I stare at my reflection—dark eyes glowing and satisfied, my maroon-painted mouth pulling up into the smallest, happiest curve. Tomorrow is looming, but right now we're here and that's enough.

I step out into the hallway to find Connor leaning against the opposite wall, arms crossed over his chest. His *bare* chest. He's wearing tuxedo pants and that's it.

"*This* is your black-tie?" I gape at him. "Jesus, you must be popular at parties."

He's too focused on my mouth to respond immediately. "Yeah, sorry, the words you just worded aren't landing."

My hands are on him before my brain can catch up. I tweak his nipple and he yelps, his shoulder banging into the wall. "I said, you're hot."

He cradles a hand over his pec, bemused. "That hurt *and* turned me on."

"Okay, put a pin in that." I slide my hand in his, pulling him toward the living room. "We have a party to get to."

OUR DECEMBER FIFTEENTH NEW YEAR'S EVE CELEBRATION IS perfect.

While I pour us champagne, Connor finds a rainbow disco light he bought years ago and forgot about, whooping gleefully. We plug it in and turn off everything else, cheers to the new year and drink one glass and then another. The lights play off his skin, turning him red like sin, blue like the melancholy I keep pushing away.

We get tipsy, punchy, drunk. The hours slip by in a blur of dancing and groping, with some photo-op breaks with his Polaroid camera and some more ill-advised karaoke. Thankfully, Connor's neighbor doesn't seem to mind this time. It could have something to do with the bottle of champagne Connor left at his door, a note tied around its neck, though he wouldn't let me read what it said. Whatever it was, it worked its magic.

"This is a top tier New Year's Eve," he says at one point. We're swaying to "Auld Lang Syne" in the middle of his living room, the disco light dancing across the walls, the pictures we took haphazardly spread out on his coffee table. Outside, it's inky black, the freezing rain turned to snow.

I rest my chin on his shoulder, watching the fat white flakes float past us, on their way to land silently three floors below. According to the news, they'll be gone by morning.

"It really is," I say. "Even though that banner's a little crook—"

His fingers dig into my ribs. "Don't start." I squirm against him with a helpless laugh and he pulls me tighter to him. His smile stretches against my cheek. "Kinda feels like we've been doing this for a long time, Claireful."

My heart skips a beat as I pull back. His eyes are heavy-lidded, his expression tender. "I know. It's weird, right?"

"It's only weird that it's not weird."

I squint. "I think even if I were sober that wouldn't make sense."

He laughs—actually, no, giggles is more accurate. The champagne's made him looser and bubbly, the human equivalent of what will now forever be my favorite drink. He's golden and light, sending effervescence through my body. This entire weekend has been a beautiful buzz.

Damn, the hangover's going to be brutal.

I tuck back into him, molding my body to his. After several beats, I whisper, "I'll miss you tomorrow."

Even for all the risks I've taken this weekend, this one is the most out of my comfort zone. It's a futile thing to say, even though it's true, because our time together doesn't change anything. I'm still going to San Francisco and he's still staying here. Trying to make a one-night—fine, three-night—stand into something more is even less realistic when distance is involved.

I *will* miss him, though, impossibly. I can't help saying it. I halfway hope he doesn't hear me.

But he does, of course. His palms smooth down my back and he presses a kiss to my temple. "I'll miss you even after that," he says and we dance, quiet now.

At 11:59, he cues up a YouTube video of a crowd counting down, then returns to me. I imagine this is how it would feel

48

even if we were in a room full of other people—like we're the only ones in it.

We count down together, confetti sticking to our bare feet, the long-gone champagne cooling in our veins.

"Happy New Year," Connor says when we hit zero. I echo it back as our lips touch, catch, come back to each other on an endless loop.

It's amazing, I think as he kisses me. This is the second year in a row where the cost of inaction has felt too massive to ignore. Where I've done something that scared me, pushed me, *changed* me. And it's the second year in a row that my heart has ached like this from the rightness of the moment, and now, from the knowledge that I'll have to leave it behind.

MONDAY IS A SHIT SHOW. MY HEAD AND HEART ARE THROBBING AS Connor's Explorer navigates to my studio so I can grab my suitcase and drop off my keys. I don't linger in the empty space—it always felt like a temporary stop between my life with Ben in the flat we shared and the life I knew I was going to get in San Francisco. It's not much of a goodbye. I don't even look back before closing the door.

Connor is subdued on our way to the airport, but manages to lead us through easy conversation. I've known him a total of sixty hours (yes, pathetically, I counted) and already I know it's unlike him. But I'm feeling it, too, and once we take our exit, we settle into silence while "Blue Christmas" plays on the radio.

The airport is an actual nightmare, snarled with cars and disgruntled people, darkening the cloud over my head.

"Shit," Connor mutters under his breath as we get caught in a line snaking toward the United departure drop-off. "I really can't do short-term parking?"

I shake my head. "A deal's a deal."

This morning while we were in bed, I told him I wanted him to drop me off at departures. Though he grumbled about it, he agreed. We got nearly three times as many hours as we agreed to when we met on Friday. I want to preserve the snow globe feeling of this whole improbable weekend. Dragging out this part will do the opposite.

Finally, we make it to the drop-off area. Connor puts on his hazards and I meet him at the trunk, watching while he hefts out my suitcase. Around us, people are scrambling. A traffic officer blows her whistle, yelling for people to keep it moving. The air bites at my cheeks and nose, but I don't move.

Connor closes the distance between us, a little tentative. His mouth is pulled down at the corners. It's so strange to see; his lips were made to curve upward. The expression looks all wrong on him.

I force a smile onto my face, like, *see? Do this.* "I think this is probably the part where I say it was nice to meet you, but that seems like an understatement."

There's the smile. It sends a flood of relief through me—and loss, too. "Well, it *was* nice to meet you." His Adam's apple bobs as he lays a palm against my cheek, his other hand curling around my waist. From somewhere nearby, the whistle shrills again. I'm pretty sure it's for us, but I don't give a shit.

His lips part and then press together before he blurts out, "I hope it's not weird for me to say I'm proud of you, because I am. You're going to do amazing things in San Francisco." His voice dips. "And holy shit am I glad I got to be the last few pages in your Portland chapter."

There's a sudden knot in my throat. "I couldn't have written them better."

"Thank you," he says, pulling me into his arms. It's tight enough that I'll feel it for hours. "I'm not kidding when I say this was the best weekend of my life."

"It was mine, too."

It was also the perfect lesson in not letting complacency mute my life. Despite my sadness, my decision to move to San Francisco feels as right as it ever has. The chance I took on Friday turned into something beautiful. I can't wait to see what's to come in my new city.

It's like he can see it in my eyes. His mouth blooms into a wide smile, identical to the first one he ever gave to me. He leans down, brushing my lips with his, nudging into my space so that we can get one last taste.

"VERY TOUCHING BUT YOU GOTTA KEEP IT MOVING!" The traffic officer yells.

Connor laughs against my mouth, then sighs. "I *would* get arrested for you. But I probably shouldn't."

"We did a good job of moving away from a life of crime on Friday," I agree.

He presses a final kiss to my forehead, squeezing my hip before stepping back. I want to cling to him. I wrap my hand around my suitcase handle instead.

"See you, Claireful," he says, backing toward his car.

"Later, Stella," I reply, backing toward the airport entrance.

He waves, grinning that sweet, goofy smile that's edged in mischief. I stole some of the Polaroids we took, but I hardly need them. That beautiful man is stamped into my brain for good.

I think I would fall in love with him if we had the time. It's scary to know that and still walk away from it.

Suddenly panicked, I blurt out, "Hey!"

Connor's head pops up over the top of his car, his expression painted with anticipation. "Hey."

My heart beats hard. It's goodbye, I know, but I can't help cracking the door open. "If you ever happen to be in the neighborhood, call me."

Something sparks in his eyes, though I can't name it from here. "Don't worry, I will."

I watch him drive away, my heart in my throat. I press a hand there and then over my chest, urging it to find its rightful place. And then I let loose a breath, turning toward my next adventure.

7

SIX MONTHS LATER

"I'M LEAVING FOR THE DAY, LEIGH," I CALL OVER MY SHOULDER, snatching my canvas bag off the wall hook near the front door. The farmers market at the Ferry Building is singing its siren song and this weekend I really can't deny it.

"Byeeeee," comes her muffled reply from her bedroom. "Hey wait, can you pick me up an eggplant and some basil if it looks good? I want to make pasta alla Norma tonight."

"I'll get you *anything* you want if you're making pasta alla Norma tonight."

Her cackle booms down the hall. "You're so easy."

"Byeeeee," I shoot back, slipping out the front door.

I'm still smiling when I fly down my apartment building stairs a minute later, buttoning my fleecy jacket while I inhale the crisp morning air. I've learned that every month in San Francisco requires a complex layer system. The weather here is like a sandwich: chilly in the morning with a several-hour window graciously allowing you to remove a specified number of layers, then cold again as soon as the sun sets. June has been more sun than fog, but I've heard July and August (or Fogust, as the locals affectionately call it) are as cold as some other city's winter.

September and October are apparently glorious, with temperatures that stretch into the eighties. I can't wait for that.

I love it here, even more than I anticipated. The company I work for is great, with a culture that genuinely encourages a healthy work-life balance. It's also a relief to be in a steady position again; if I discovered anything this year, it's that freelance work isn't for the faint of heart.

Meanwhile, Leigh, a good friend in college, has proven herself to be an even better one now. Our apartment in Russian Hill is quiet and cozy, the perfect place to come home to when I'm done with my day. We binge TV shows together and switch off cooking duties when the mood strikes, but we also give each other plenty of space to live our own lives. Her group of friends have become mine, but I've also made some on my own through my job. The happy hours are abundant, as are the brunches and the park picnics and the weekend day trips (usually up to Napa, truthfully).

My life feels significantly fuller than it did in Portland. More importantly, it feels like mine.

When my family came to visit last month, Tristan pulled me back as we trudged down a trail at Land's End. My parents and Gavin wandered ahead, caught up in their conversation.

"You look happy," he said, peering at me with dark eyes that matched mine. "Like, really settled and content."

"I am," I replied, surprised he could see it.

He nodded slowly, thoughtful, then laughed. "Jeez, imagine if you were still with that nerd."

"*You're* a nerd," I shot back, but the truth is, I did imagine it. Especially at the beginning, I thought often about my life in Portland—the good and the bad, the ways in which I'd grown. The ways in which I'd risked discomfort and sadness to become more settled in myself, and how it had rewarded me.

But most of all, I thought about Connor. I've replayed that weekend so many times that the mental tape is worn from use. I can still hear his voice in my ear whispering how good it was. Can still feel his keen attention while I talked, can feel him moving in me, gripping my hips hard, biting at my neck. I can see that mischievous smile and those honey eyes, immortalized in my memory and also in the Polaroids we took, which are lovingly tucked into an old romance book. I miss him in a way I never, ever missed Ben.

It shouldn't make sense, but that's how it was from the start. All those things Connor and I experienced that weekend were improbable and yet they were more real than anything I've felt before or since.

I blink out of that thought as a MUNI bus comes screeching to a halt beside me. I didn't even realize I'd made it to my bus stop; I walked here in a stupor.

Ahead of me, a man queues up to board. I can't see his face, but I can tell he's around my age. He's brown-haired and tall, his fingers tapping out an impatient beat on his thigh.

I've done so many double takes in this city thanks to men who look like Connor. They're absolutely crawling all over San Francisco. They're boarding buses and strolling out of bars. They're at my coffee place every morning and walking their dogs. None of them are him, of course, but it doesn't stop me from searching.

At first I thought I was just latching onto the idea of him in my new city, the echo of his dream job still ringing in my ears. But when I confessed to Leigh that I was worried I was obsessed, she waved me off.

"You can't walk six feet without tripping over a handsome white guy with brown hair. There are a million of them."

Oddly, it turned into an inside joke between Connor and me, starting when I texted him a few weeks after I'd left. We never discussed whether we'd keep in touch, but Connor sent me random messages from the start—making sure I'd settled in okay, texting me that he was still thinking about adopting that cat he'd mentioned.

One morning, I took a sly picture of a guy holding a carrier outside a vet's office. I sent it to Connor and tacked on:

Is this you and Jimbo?

He replied immediately.

Nope, but this is

Seconds later I got a picture of him and a gorgeous tabby cat with wide green eyes that broadcasted his dissatisfaction with being squished into a selfie. I gasped, zooming in on the picture to devour all the Connor-specific things that made me ache in memory before I wrote back.

You got him!!!!

I got him. I'm in love. He's playing it real cool, but I'm confident I won't get ghosted

You two look dangerously adorable together

His response came a few minutes later. I watched my screen, text bubbles popping up and then stopping in a seemingly endless loop until he said:

Wish that guy WAS me, though

It's possible I kept texting him pictures of random men because I wanted him to keep saying that, which he did. But I haven't done it lately. It makes me wish for things I can't have and anyway, our sporadic texts have gotten even more irregular these past few weeks. I've started wondering if he's seeing someone.

The thought makes my stomach lurch. Maybe that's why I sneak a picture of this guy now, capturing the shoulders that aren't quite as broad as Connor's, hair that doesn't flop onto his forehead, hips that aren't quite as lean.

It's impulsive and completely futile to text him, but I just can't let him go.

Is this you?

Almost immediately, my phone lights up. I gasp. Connor Stella is *calling me*. For a second, I freeze; Connor and I only text. A phone call is a very unexpected level-up.

I eye the bus. Everyone's boarded, Not Connor included.

Oh, fuck it, I'll get the next one. My fingers fumble to answer. "Hello?"

"I swear you're psychic. I was just about to call you."

Connor's voice is rich and playful in my ear. I grin, my heart taking off. "I can tell, Mr. Trigger Finger. My text went through half a second ago."

"You and your number inflation issues, Claireful. I waited a respectable three."

"*You're* the one inflating the number this time, sir."

"You *de*flated the number for drama purposes, ma'am," he shoots back. "You knew exactly what you were doing."

I hum, grinning up at the blue sky. My heart feels like it's about to beat out of my chest. "Let's call a truce and settle on two point five."

"Deal," he says, his voice low and happy. There's a pause, like he's holding his breath. I know I'm holding mine. "But, actually, it really was half a second. And I really was about to call you."

"To what do I owe the honor?"

"Well," he says, "you told me to let you know if I was ever in the neighborhood."

I swear my vision goes spotty for a second, a near-brush with a swoon. "Are—you're in San Francisco?"

The grin in his voice is clear, but there's an undercurrent of uncertainty, too. "I am. I know it's short notice, but I was hoping I could steal you away for a drink or dinner tonight."

"A drink or food or whatever?" I tease. It's a callback to that first night we met, the small act of bravery he made in asking me out, not knowing that I was planning the same thing. A risk that paid dividends.

"Yeah, any of that," he says, a breathless huff of laughter chasing the word. I wonder if he's remembering, too. I wonder if he replays that weekend as much as I do. "Or all of it, honestly."

"Yes." I don't even have to think about it. The word is out of my mouth before my brain can process what it could possibly mean that he's here, that he called me, that he wants to see me. I have no idea what will happen tonight. But I didn't six months ago either, and that turned into something that I still can't let go of.

"Really?" His voice lifts an octave, like it's weightless with relief.

"Really," I say. "Just tell me where to meet you and I'll be there."

8

My Uber leaves me bewildered on the sidewalk in NoPa just after eight. I stare up at a nondescript apartment building, which is surrounded by similar apartment buildings, their bay windows alive with golden light and movement.

This is strange.

Connor texted me the address earlier, and in my excitement and discombobulation over getting to see him imminently, I didn't think to check its accuracy. He must have transposed some numbers or something—there are tons of restaurants and bars in this neighborhood, but they're several blocks away.

"What the hell," I mutter, shooting him a questioning text before turning on my heel to start walking toward Divisadero Street.

I'm halfway down the block when a tall figure, dressed in jeans and a sweater, turns the corner. His head is bowed, a bottle of wine in one hand, a bouquet of flowers in the other.

Is it him? I think, playing the same game I have for the past six months as my steps instinctively quicken.

I don't need to play it tonight, though—my body gets it before my brain kicks in. Before he lifts his head. Before that honey gaze, muted in the evening night, locks with mine and I see the same beautiful, wide smile that snared me six months ago spreading across his mouth.

It's Connor Stella in the beautiful flesh.

There's no time to wonder if touching him after so long apart, when who knows what we even are to each other anymore, is appropriate. I'm in his arms two seconds later. Smelling the spice of his skin, then pressing my nose against it, right where his pulse beats heavily in his neck. Behind my back, the *clink* of glass echoes—the wine bottle hitting the logo buckle on my purse—and for a beat I'm transported back to the alley that December night back in Portland, when I was surrounded by bottles and grinning up at Connor.

The same Connor who has his arms tight around me now, grinning down at *me*.

My body unfurls against the heat of him, my heart beating double time. The six months between us disappears when he murmurs, "Hey, Claireful."

"Hey, Stella," I whisper back, overwhelmed as I step out of his hold. I'm not going to be able to form words if I'm touching him in any way. As it is, I barely manage a stuttered, "I was—where—I just texted you."

Connor bites his lip, his eyes wandering over my face with amusement and something sweeter. "Sorry, I was around the corner at Bi-Rite picking up some provisions."

"The important ones, I see," I say, eyeing the wine's sky-blue label, then the flowers still clutched in his hand. It's a gorgeous spray of wildflowers in blushing pink; the same color as my cheeks, probably.

God, he's more gorgeous than I remember. Tall and handsome as hell, hair ruffling in the breeze that's currently pulling a blanket of fog over the city.

He rocks forward on his heels like he's going to bring me against his body again, but catches himself, instead holding up the flowers so I can take them. "I covered the 'drink' and 'whatever' portion of the evening in one fell swoop."

I raise an eyebrow, remembering what the 'whatever' portion of our evening consisted of last time. It definitely wasn't flowers. He grins back, blushing a little, and lifts an eyebrow, like, *we could do that, too.*

God, I hope so, but first—

"Now that the provisions are all squared away, maybe you can solve a mystery for me, because I'm confused." I look around, gesturing to the apartment buildings lining each side of the street for at least two blocks. "Did you get the address wrong?"

"Nope," he says, his smile growing mischievous, though it's edged in anxiety.

I blink at him. "This is an apartment building."

He looks up, appraising it as he scratches at his cheek, before turning back to me. "Yep."

Now it's not my body unfurling, but suspicion—and a vicious hope. "What's happening right now?"

For a second, he doesn't say anything, just gazes at me like he's drinking me in. Then he swallows. "Can I show you?"

All I can do is nod and follow him. He punches in a code on the call box, pushing the front door open when it buzzes and leading me toward a winding set of stairs. I'm out of breath by the time we get to the fourth floor, my heart pounding hard at the exertion and also at what all of this means.

Connor doesn't touch me, but he looks over his shoulder no less than a dozen times to make sure I'm still with him as we make our way down the hall, his smile shy. It obliterates me. Having him in front of me now makes me realize just how intensely I missed him. I want to put my hands all over him just to reassure myself he's real, he's here.

He's *here.*

We stop at the last door on the left and Connor unlocks it. As soon as the door creaks open, a head pops out, wide green eyes staring up at me.

"*Jimbo*?" I gasp, turning to Connor.

His shoulders pull up into a bashful shrug. "You told me to call when I was in the neighborhood. Well, as of last week, I'm in this neighborhood. Uh, permanently, though."

I throw myself at him, wrapping my arms around his neck so tightly that he lets out a strangled laugh. "Oh, my god," I whisper against his cheek. "You got your dream job."

"I got it," he says, pressing his face into the curve of my shoulder. He inhales, then lets loose a sigh that's steeped in relief, his hands moving up and down my back in slow sweeps.

"I'm so proud of you." I pull back, taking in the flush rushing across his cheeks, pushing its way down his neck.

"Claire..." He trails off, his voice hoarse with a longing I recognize in myself. "I meant what I said before, that me being here doesn't mean you owe me anything. Not even a drink or food or whatever, and certainly not more than that. But—"

"I need you to shut up." I cover his mouth. His eyes widen and then crinkle, his lips curling against my palm. "I've spent the last six months texting you pictures of random men, wanting it to be *you*."

"That was an occasionally offensive game," he says behind my hand.

"It was bound to be. No one can live up to the real Connor Stella," I agree with more levity than I feel. There's a knot in my throat—my heart, too, maybe.

He circles my wrist, kissing my palm softly before pulling my hand down, his gaze locked with mine. "I was going to wait to fully settle in before calling you, but I couldn't. I haven't been able to stop thinking about you since I dropped you off at the airport. It was only a weekend, but it felt like everything, didn't it?"

The knot grows. Below us, Jimbo snakes around my ankles and then Connor's, meowing.

I think about those small decisions we made that night—smiling at one another across the bar, talking in the alley, the promise of drinks that turned into sex and more. Even now, I sometimes get caught up in the risk and reward of the big decisions I make, like moving here. But the small ones matter, too. When you collect them in your hand over time, they grow just as massive. Connor and I are a testament to that.

I don't even have to think about what the cost of inaction would be now. He's holding his heart out with no expectations for mine. It makes me want to give him all of it.

"I have some bad news," I say, stepping closer.

Connor's hopeful expression dims slightly. "Hit me with it."

"You owe me."

His eyebrows pull together in confusion, even as his mouth twitches. "What do I owe you?"

Wrapping myself around him like I'm Jimbo, I curve into all the little hollows I'll grow to learn. His hands go to my hips as I stretch up, whispering in his ear, "More of that everything you said you felt. I felt it, too, and you can't live in my city and not pay up."

I feel his smile against my cheek, then see it when he leans back to meet my eyes. "I promise I'm good for it."

His mouth on mine is the period at the end of that sentence, but it also feels the beginning of some sort of promise. He cradles my face as he pushes me against the door frame, fitting his body to mine so there's no space between us. His thumb passes over my cheek, his soft sigh parting my lips so he can take the kiss deeper. I groan quietly when his tongue slides against mine and he sighs again, a happy sound I can taste on my tongue.

"Have we officially reached the 'whatever' portion of the evening?" I murmur against his mouth.

He drags his lips down to my jaw, presses an open-mouthed kiss just below my ear. "We haven't even done the drinks or food part."

"Later," I say, gripping his sweater, and he whispers back, "yeah," pushing me into his apartment.

The door slams behind us, which sends Jimbo shooting off toward the living room. I laugh, but Connor is focused now, grazing his mouth over mine once and then again, a slow back and forth that pulls a beautiful burn onto my lips. He soothes it with the firm, damp press of his mouth, with his tongue. His low groan rumbles against me while our hands move everywhere, remembering so easily how we did this before.

"Jesus, this *dress*." He says it like he's in pain, gripping the ribbed knit fabric, pulling it up until the hem is at my hips instead of my ankles. He looks down between us, his lashes fanning against his cheeks, then smiles sweetly at me, hooking a finger into the waistband of my underwear. "I like it better like this."

"Of course you do. I'm more naked this way," I reply breathlessly.

"You could be nakeder, though."

"I don't think that's a word."

His brows pull together in mock reproach, though it's undermined by the hungry curve of his mouth. "We'll consult the dictionary later, Claire."

I laugh, but it's short-lived as Connor crowds into my space, trapping me against the wall, his finger still hooked into my underwear.

We watch together, breath held, as his hand disappears behind the lace. The way his knuckles stretch the fabric, how I can't see him but I can *feel* him, is almost obscene. My moan dominoes into his when he feels what he's done to me, and he curls his free hand around the nape of my neck, pulling my mouth to his.

"Mmm. I love it here already," he murmurs just before he kisses me. Just before he circles his fingers over me, paints me with the wetness there, slides his fingers lower and then inside. He stokes my need so high that it's less than ten seconds before I'm fumbling with the zipper of his jeans.

We don't make it to the bedroom. I don't even know if he *has* one, or if this is a studio, or if there are any walls other than the one he's got me pinned against. It all happens too fast—I'm kicking off my underwear, gripping the stiff length of him, moving my hand in the same cadence he's moving his, and he's groaning into my neck, pulling a condom from his wallet— "another provision, very wishful on my part" he pants with a grin. Then we're giggling into a kiss, and another and another, until it melts into something too necessary to laugh at. But it still feels joyful, warm and honey-like, a feeling that's the same color as his eyes, somehow, which are latched to mine as he slides inside me.

Groaning, he grips my thighs, cinches them tight around his hips. Bites at my bottom lip and then licks at it, into my mouth. Kisses me just as deeply as he pushes into my body.

I feel each second of those six months we didn't spend together. And with Connor's mouth pressed against my neck, with the way he whispers my name when I come minutes later, I feel our dedication to make up for every single one of them.

CONNOR DOES ACTUALLY HAVE A BEDROOM, SO WE MIGRATE THERE once we've fed ourselves.

"I want to hear about how you got the job," I say, curling up against him in bed, my thigh slung over his. It's a strange comfort to see the same furniture I took stock of back in December, the same stack of books. The Polaroid camera we'll put to good use at some point.

He hums, pulling me closer as he presses a kiss to the crown of my head. "We skipped that part, huh?"

"We had other important business to attend to," I say, and his mouth curls up against my hair. A smirk, no doubt, even though I can't see it to confirm. "But now I'm ready to hear all the dirty details of your journey to becoming a San Francisco resident."

He tells me about the day he got the notice for the job listing, how hard his hands shook as he applied. He laughs recalling his first call with Theo, how he was so nervous that he called him Mr. Spencer and Theo replied sharply, "Jesus, *no*. That's my dad" and he was sure he'd fucked it up. He tells me about the second-round phone call and how he went all in, pitching his skillset and passion for Theo's company. By the end of the call, he'd been offered the job.

"I love Theo Spencer," I say, propping myself up on an elbow.

"Shit, me too," Connor says with a laugh. I open my mouth and then close it, biting my lip. He reaches up, pushes my hair behind my ear, murmuring, "What is it?"

"I wondered if you'd met someone," I admit. "These past few weeks, I mean. Not that we were prolific texters anyway, but I didn't really hear from you."

His eyebrows crash together and he makes an apologetic sound as he pulls me on top of him. "I was scrambling with all the moving logistics, but more than that, I knew that if we texted too much, I'd blurt it all out."

"Why'd you wait until you got here to tell me?"

His hands make an absent circuit along my hips, up my back and down again. He gazes up at the ceiling, gathering his thoughts before focusing back on me. "I guess I was nervous about what your response would be. I didn't want to encroach on your space, you know? This is your adventure, Claireful."

I love the way he says it, like that name makes up all of the things I am now and what I haven't become yet. Like he wants all of it. I may be a reformed careful girl, but the safety in that knowledge does something irrevocable to my heart.

"Now it's your adventure, too," I say quietly.

His smile echoes my tone. "Yeah."

"I'm really good at sharing," I promise.

His expression melts into something that could easily slip into love, now that we have the time to get there. "Is that your adorable way of saying you want this, too?"

"I already told you," I say, just before he pulls me down for a kiss. "I want everything."

ACKNOWLEDGMENTS

This novelette was supposed to be a very short story. It was also never supposed to see the light of day. My brain was fully shriveled after writing *You, with a View* and I wanted to jump into a quick project to prove to myself that I could still, in fact, write *something*. Anything!

I wrote it over the course of a few weeks during the holidays in 2021/early 2022, and it turned into a straightforwardly joyful experience. There were zero expectations, no pressure to ever show it to anyone—it was just me and Claire and Connor, stuck in an apartment for a few days while the world beyond it was quiet. I ended up with a story that was 15k longer than I anticipated ("I'll keep it to 5k max!" the overwriter deluded herself), a story that was fun and steamy and yeah, a little melancholy because if nothing else, I carry a little piece of the spirit of Phoebe Bridgers inside of me. I can't apologize for that!!

So, it really *wasn't* meant to be anything other than a story that I occasionally peddled to my friends.

Except, this year people started reading YWAV. And they started saying "I can't WAIT for your next book." And they started asking when that would be, and getting bummed out when I told them it'd be another year. And the thing is, I love the people who read my work so immensely, and I also love surprises and giving people presents. Publishing this novelette was the best of both those things—a way to be a little Machiavellian (I've been giggling nonstop about surprising you all with this) and a way to say thank you for wanting more of my work.

(You see what I mean about overwriting?? Why are these acknowledgments so long?? Someone take the mic away from me!)

As for the rest of my thank yous: first to Livy Hart, Laya Brusi, and Sarah T. Dubb for being the best critique partners in the game. I started writing this for myself, then threw it in their laps, and they read it with their ever-kind and keen eyes.

Thank you to my agent, Samantha Fabien, for reading this when I had no plans for it, and for helping me clear the path when I did. Thank you to Kerry Donovan and team for saying "go for it!" when I wanted to get this out in time for the holidays.

Thank you to everyone who's read any iteration of this book: Mazey Eddings (also for providing a blurb, what an icon); Regina Black; Alicia Thompson; Nicole Poulsen; Mae Bennett; Ava Watson; Lindsay Grossman; Andrea; Hailey; Lindsey; Jen; Elsie; and Sofia. If I forgot anyone, forgive me because I know I sent this to people back in 2021 and I have a terrible memory. It's my ADHD. Please love me through it!!

Thank you to Tarah and Laya for answering my endless number of self-pub questions; if I f*cked anything up it's 100% on me. And thank you to Anita Kelly for helping me with a few Portland-related details!

Thank you to Lavanya and Kate for always reading my stuff over the past many, many years, even when it's half formed or terrible. You are the OGs and my best friend equivalent of the song "New Year's Day."

Thank you to my little fam. There's no one I'd rather count down to midnight on New Year's Eve with.

Thank you to Taylor Swift, always, whose songs have, do, and will forevermore crowd my playlists.

And finally, again, thank YOU. Thank you for wanting to read the books I write. Thank you for your support. Thank you for showing up for me ALL the time. The best people read my work, and I will stand by that until the end of time.

ABOUT THE AUTHOR

 Jessica Joyce lives happily-ever-ongoing with her husband and son in the Bay Area. When she's not writing character-driven, realistic and relatable tales of millennials who are just Doing Their Best while falling in love, you can find her listening to one of her dozens of chaotically curated Spotify playlists, trying out a new skincare face mask, crying over cute animal TikToks, or watching the 2005 version of *Pride & Prejudice*.

Printed in Dunstable, United Kingdom